Lulu Bell and the

Pyjama Party

A Random House book
Published by Random House Australia Pty Ltd
Level 3, 100 Pacific Highway, North Sydney NSW 2060
www.randomhouse.com.au

First published by Random House Australia in 2014

Addresses for companies within the Random House Group can be found at
www.randomhouse.com.au/offices

National Library of Australia
Cataloguing-in-Publication Entry

Author: Murrell, Belinda
Title: Lulu Bell and the pyjama party/Belinda Murrell; illustrated by Serena Geddes
ISBN: 978 0 85798 303 9 (paperback)
Series: Murrell, Belinda. Lulu Bell; 8
Target audience: For primary school age
Subjects: Children's parties – Juvenile fiction
            Sleepovers – Juvenile fiction
            Dogs – Juvenile fiction
Other authors/contributors: Geddes, Serena
Dewey number: A823.4

Cover and internal illustrations by Serena Geddes
Cover design by Christabella Designs
Internal design and typesetting in 16/22 pt Bembo by Anna Warren, Warren Ventures
Printed in Australia by Griffin Press, an accredited ISO AS/NZS 14001:2004
Environmental Management System printer

Lulu Bell and the Pyjama Party

Belinda Murrell

Illustrated by Serena Geddes

RANDOM HOUSE AUSTRALIA

Molly   Tien and Sam   Lulu

Dad   Mum   Gus   Rosie

For two beautiful nieces –
Meg and Lauren

Chapter 1

Saturday Morning

It was early when Lulu Bell opened her eyes. She nearly rolled over and went back to sleep, but then she remembered. It was Saturday morning – hurray! Lulu loved Saturdays. And this was to be a very special one, because Mum had organised a pyjama party.

Lulu's best friend Molly was coming to stay. So was her little brother Sam.

Even Ebony the kitten was coming for the sleepover.

Lulu jumped out of bed. Lulu's sister Rosie was still asleep in the bed opposite, her dark hair fanned out on the pillow.

Lulu got dressed quickly and quietly. Saturday was also soccer day, so Lulu pulled on her team uniform. There was a sky-blue soccer shirt, white shorts, shin pads and long blue socks.

She picked up her soccer boots and ran into the kitchen.

Lulu's mum was sitting at the table and reading the newspaper.

'Good morning, honey bun,' said
Mum. 'Did you have a lovely sleep?'

Her dad was at the kitchen bench.

'How's my little soccer star?' asked
Dad. 'Are you ready for the big game
against the Mighty Sharks?'

Lulu gave them both a good morning
hug as she answered their questions.
She stood behind the
kitchen bench and
helped Dad crack eggs
into a bowl.

Next Dad sliced up mushrooms for the omelette. Dad and Lulu always made a special breakfast on Saturday mornings.

Lulu looked at the clock on the kitchen wall. Her brown eyes danced with excitement.

'What time are they coming?' she asked.

She whisked the eggs with a little milk.

'It's seven o'clock,' said Mum. 'Molly and Sam should be here any minute.'

Just then the doorbell rang.

'They're here,' cried Lulu.

She raced to the front door, followed by two brown dogs.

Outside stood Molly, Sam and their mum Tien. They were carrying their sleeping bags and pillows. Molly was also dressed in her sky-blue soccer uniform.

Tien was holding a small carry cage
and two overnight bags. One of Lulu's
dogs, Jessie, sniffed at the cage.

Meow, cried a cross voice from inside. Ebony the kitten didn't like being sniffed at.

'Hello, Molly,' cried Lulu. 'Hello, Tien and Sam. Come in.'

'Hello, Lulu,' said Molly and Tien together.

Tien was dressed in her high heels and a suit. She was going away for the weekend for work.

Sam didn't say anything. He looked up at Lulu with big, dark eyes. He held his mum's hand tightly.

Everyone came inside. Mum welcomed them.

'Put your pillows and sleeping bags in the lounge room,' suggested Mum. 'I thought you could all sleep in there tonight in front of the fire.'

'Mum said we can toast some

marshmallows over the fire,' said Lulu. 'Just like camping.'

Molly and Lulu stacked the bedding neatly near the sofa. Rosie and Gus came in then. All the commotion had woken them up. Gus rubbed his eyes and yawned.

Dad popped his head around the door to say hello. Sam looked around at all the people and shrank closer to his mother's side.

'Do you have time for a cup of tea?' Mum asked Tien.

Tien checked her watch. 'No, I have to get going,' she replied. 'Thanks so much for having the children for me. I don't know what I'd have done without you.'

'It's a pleasure,' replied Mum. 'You know we love having Molly, Sam and Ebony any time.'

Sam buried his face against his mother's skirt. Tien hugged him close. She lowered her voice.

'Sam's feeling a little shy,' explained Tien. 'He's never stayed away from home before.'

Lulu came over to Sam. She threw her honey-coloured plait over her shoulder and crouched down beside him.

'Don't worry, Sam,' said Lulu. 'We're going to have so much fun. We have

soccer this morning. Then we can play games and eat party food. You'll love it, I promise.'

Sam looked up at Lulu. He blinked behind his glasses. Lulu thought he might start crying. She tried to think of something to cheer him up.

'Do you think Ebony is excited about having a sleepover at her mum's house?' asked Lulu.

Ebony was one of Pickles's kittens. She had been born in the washing machine. Now she lived with Molly and Sam.

Sam nodded slowly.

'Shall we go and look for Pickles then?' asked Lulu. 'I think she might be hiding somewhere. Let's hope she isn't in the washing machine this time!'

Mum smiled at Lulu. 'Great idea, honey bun. But first, Sam, give your mum a kiss goodbye.'

Sam and Molly kissed Tien goodbye. Tien hugged them both, looking worried. Mum walked Tien towards the front door.

'Sam will be fine,' said Mum. 'We'll look after him.'

Lulu took Sam's hand.

'Come on, Sam. Let's find Pickles!'

Chapter 2

The Hunt for Pickles

Molly opened the carry cage and scooped out Ebony. The velvety black kitten purred and rubbed her face against Molly's chin.

'Sam, would you like to carry Ebony?' asked Molly.

Sam nodded and took the kitten in his arms. He hugged her close.

Lulu led the way. The five children hunted for Pickles in all the usual spots.

Jessie tagged along, sniffing and searching. They looked in Dad's shoe cupboard, on the back step and under the lavender bush. On the way, they stopped to say hello to Flopsy the bunny and the ducklings in their run.

They even checked in the washing machine, just in case. But Pickles wasn't there.

Finally Rosie found Pickles, the tortoiseshell cat, curled up under Lulu's bed.

Ebony leaped out of Sam's arms and raced to her mother. Pickles meowed and licked her kitten on the head. Ebony purred with pleasure.

The children lay on the floor and watched the cat reunion under the bed. Ebony snuggled against her mother and butted her with her head. Pickles put her

paw on Ebony. She held her kitten down
and washed her face with her rough
tongue. Ebony squirmed and wriggled as
she was licked all over.

'Aren't they cute?' asked Lulu. 'Pickles
is giving her a bath.'

Rosie screwed up her face. 'I'm glad
Mum doesn't lick me when she gives me
a bath,' she said.

Lulu laughed.

'Ebony loves seeing her mother,' said Molly.

At the mention of the word mother, Sam pushed his glasses back on his nose and gave a little sniffle.

'It's all right, Sam,' said Molly.

'When is Mum coming back?' asked Sam. His voice cracked. 'I don't like her going away.'

'She'll be here tomorrow afternoon,' said Molly.

Sam pushed his bottom lip out, trying not to cry. Lulu thought for a moment. *Poor Sam. How can I help him feel better?*

'Sam, your mum doesn't want to go away,' said Lulu. 'But sometimes people have to do things they don't want to do. Sometimes we have to be a little bit brave.'

'Bug Boy brave,' said Gus.

He pushed his bug boy mask back off his face. His antennae wobbled.

'Can you be brave, Sam?' asked Lulu.

Sam thought about it. 'I'm brave too,' he decided.

'Good,' said Lulu. 'Let's go and eat some breakfast.'

They all sat around the kitchen table. Dad served the cheesy ham-and-mushroom omelette on toast. It was delicious.

Everyone chatted and laughed as they ate. Except Sam.

He pushed his fork around the plate.

'Not hungry, Sam?' asked Mum.
'Don't worry. If you can't finish your
breakfast, the dogs will love it.'

The dogs lay on their bed in the
corner. At the mention of breakfast,
both of them sat up and thumped their
tails. It was easy to tell them apart. Asha's
muzzle was grey, while her daughter
Jessie was the smiliest dog in the world.

After breakfast, the kids cleared
the table. Mum and Rosie stacked the
dishwasher. Lulu showed Sam how to
feed the dogs.

'Sit, girls,' ordered Lulu. Asha and
Jessie sat obediently, their tongues
hanging out. 'Stay.'

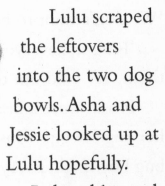

Lulu scraped
the leftovers
into the two dog
bowls. Asha and
Jessie looked up at
Lulu hopefully.

Lulu whispered
to Sam. 'Now say,
"good girls". That's
how they know
they're allowed to eat.
We've trained them to
have beautiful manners.'

Sam looked at the two big dogs. Asha thumped her tail on the floor. 'Good girls,' he said.

The two dogs leapt up. They gobbled up their breakfast in seconds and licked the bowls clean. Sam smiled.

'Now we'd better get going,' said Dad. 'We don't want to be late for the game.'

'Rug up, everyone,' Mum reminded them. 'It's cold out there.'

Rosie wore a beanie and scarf with her angel wings. Gus pulled down his bug boy mask. Everyone grabbed a warm jacket.

It was a fifteen-minute walk to Lagoon Park. The dogs bounded along, sniffing all the wonderful smells. They loved coming to soccer on Saturday mornings too. Mum had the water bottles and the sliced oranges in a container. Dad had his whistle and the soccer ball.

There were lots of families arriving at the park. Some of the kids wore the same sky-blue uniform as Lulu and Molly. Others wore the black and red of the opposition – the Mighty Sharks. Lulu felt a bubble of excitement well up. She loved soccer.

'Come on, Gus. Come on, Sam. Let's go. It's time for some super Squid fun.'

Chapter 3

The Shelly Beach Squids

Lulu and Molly ran over to join their team mates — the Shelly Beach Squids. Lots of Lulu's best friends from school were on the team. As well as Molly, there was Lauren, Thomas and Flynn, plus the twins, Olivia and Jo.

'Hi, Lulu,' called Lauren. 'Hi, Molly.'

'Lauren, how's Maisie?' asked Lulu. Maisie was Lauren's black Labrador. She was going to have puppies any day now.

'Big and slow,' replied Lauren with a grin. 'Mum said we should bring her in for a check-up with your dad today.'

'I hope she has the puppies really soon,' said Lulu. 'Labrador puppies are so chubby and wrinkly. They'll be adorable.'

'Come on, girls,' called the coach, waving her arms. She gave Lulu a special smile.

The Squids' coach was Kylie the vet nurse. Kylie was a star soccer player. The Squids gathered around. Lulu jumped up and down to keep warm, and tucked her hands under her armpits.

Mum hurried over with her clipboard and pen. She was the team manager. She made sure the players swapped over regularly so everyone got a turn to play.

Dad was the referee, with his whistle

and cap. He helped Kylie to warm the kids up before the game.

The Squids jogged up and down the football field. They skipped sideways, stretched and sprinted. They practised passing the ball and tackling. Then Kylie gave them some last-minute reminders before the game began.

'Remember to spread out,' said Kylie. 'Pass the ball and kick hard.'

Rosie, Gus and Sam stood on the sideline with all the other families. Rosie held Asha's lead while Sam held Jessie's lead.

Then Dad blew the whistle to start the game. The two teams chased the ball. They kicked it back and forth. Flynn was the goalkeeper for the first half. He had to try to stop the other team from scoring. The others chased the ball, trying to shoot it towards their own goal net.

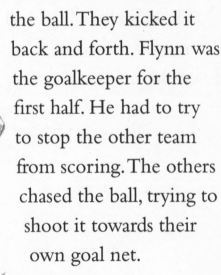

It was a very exciting game. Thomas loved doing tricks with his feet, flipping the ball in the air. The ball came close and Lulu kicked it with all her might. The ball shot down the other end of the field.

'Great kick, Lulu,' yelled Mum from the sideline.

Thomas chased the ball and moved it further down the field.

He passed it to Lauren. Lauren gave a super-big kick. The ball flew over the goalkeeper's head and into the back of the net.

'Goal,' yelled Thomas. He punched the air.

Everyone ran down to give Lauren a hug.

A few minutes later, the Mighty Sharks scored a goal. It was one goal for each side.

Then it was half-time. Mum passed out the container of orange pieces. Dad handed out the water bottles. Lulu had a long drink of water.

'Great work, Squids,' said Kylie. 'That was an awesome goal by Lauren and great passing by Thomas.'

Kylie patted Lauren on the shoulder. 'Keep up the good work, team.'

Dad blew the whistle. It was time to

start playing again. For this half, Molly was the goalkeeper. The Squids played hard and finally scored another goal.

'Two goals to one,' called Mum from the sideline.

Rosie clapped. Gus was lying on the ground with his head on Asha's tummy. Jessie sat beside him watching the ball shoot back and forth. Sam was picking blades of grass.

The other team huddled together whispering.

Dad blew the whistle. Lulu kicked the ball to Flynn. Flynn sent it flying towards the net. Lulu thought they would score another goal. But the Sharks grabbed the ball and kicked it back down the field.

Lauren ran in for a daring tackle. The Sharks were too quick for her. Then Thomas got the ball for a moment, but

it was stolen back by the Sharks. They
scooted up the other end to score a goal
over Molly's head. It was two goals each.

'Come on, Squids,' yelled Kylie. 'Grab
the ball. Just a few minutes to go.'

Rosie and her friend Mia were
standing on the sideline.

'Go Lulu, go Squids,' Rosie chanted. She waved her arms in the air.

'Go Squidses,' shouted Gus. He leaped up and down.

Sam jumped to his feet. Jessie barked with excitement. Her lead dropped to the ground.

The ball came bounding down the field. Lulu got to it first. She ran along, dribbling the ball with her feet. A Shark came in to tackle Lulu. She quickly passed the ball to Lauren.

Jessie bounded along the sideline. Her tongue was hanging out and her tail was wagging. Sam jammed his glasses back against his nose and hurtled after the dog.

Lauren charged forward. She paused, took careful aim and then kicked, straight towards the goal.

Jessie darted onto the field, chasing the ball. She ran straight in front of the goal nets and knocked over the Sharks' goalkeeper. The ball sailed into the back of the net. Lauren jumped in the air. Jessie barked.

'Great goal, Lauren,' called Thomas.

Jessie licked the Sharks' goalkeeper all over his face.

'Jessie,' shouted Lulu. 'Naughty girl.'

'That's not fair,' cried one of the Sharks' players. 'The dog knocked the goalie over.'

Jessie sat in the middle of the goal posts with a big doggy smile. The Shark goalie stood up. He wiped his face on his sleeve.

Dad blew the whistle. It was full-time.

'We won,' shouted Flynn. A cheer went up from the Squids. The players from the Mighty Sharks scowled.

'Not so fast, Flynn,' said Dad.

Everyone looked at Dad. He pushed his cap back on his head.

'I'm sorry, Lauren,' said Dad. 'I can't allow that goal. There was interference from the spectators – well, from Jessie.'

Lulu felt her stomach sink. She hoped no-one would be angry with Jessie.

Sam watched Dad with worried eyes.

Lauren looked at Jessie. Jessie smiled back, her ears cocked. Lauren grinned.

'That's okay, Dr Bell,' said Lauren. 'I think Jessie loves soccer as much as I do.'

Everyone laughed. Sam smiled too. Lulu felt the weight lift from her tummy. She gave Lauren a hug.

'So it's a draw between the Shelly Beach Squids and the Mighty Sharks,' said Dad.

The Mighty Sharks cheered. All the kids crowded around Jessie. They patted her and joked about her dash. Jessie wagged her tail. She looked very pleased with herself.

'Oh, Jessie,' scolded Lulu. 'You're not supposed to run onto the field.'

Jessie licked Lulu's hand to say sorry.

Lulu hugged her back. She couldn't be cross with Jessie for long.

'Never mind, Lulu,' said Mum. 'It was still a great game.'

Chapter 4

Nika

 After the soccer game, all the parents crowded around. Kylie listed the best moments in the game, and praised all the kids. Lauren won the Player of the Match trophy. She would keep it for the week. Lauren's parents and her little brother Justin beamed proudly.

Then it was time to go home.

At home, Gus and Sam played superheroes. Gus zoomed around the

garden, pretending he could fly. His
cloak swirled behind him. Sam followed
him, wearing a tablecloth tied over his
shoulders. Jessie chased them in circles,
her ears flapping like wings.

Mum helped Rosie to sort through
the dress-up box. Rosie *oohed* and *aahed*
over ball gowns, pirate swords and
witches hats. Ebony pounced on a scrap
of white lace, tumbling and rolling.

'Molly, would you like to come next door and help Dad for a while?' asked Lulu.

Lulu and her family lived in the rambling old house behind the Shelly Beach vet hospital. Saturdays were always busy, with lots of animal patients to see. Lulu loved to help out.

'Yes, please,' said Molly. 'There's always so much going on there.'

Lulu pushed open the thick green door that separated the Bells' home from the vet hospital in front. Immediately she could smell the tangy odour of antiseptic and animals.

In the very front of the vet hospital was the waiting room. It was crowded with people and pets. There were cats and bunnies in carry cages, and dogs on leads.

Kylie was sitting at the desk talking

to a client. She had changed out of her
soccer coach outfit. Now she wore her
crisp blue vet nurse's uniform.

The client had a funny-shaped
bundle in her arms. It was wrapped in a
white towel. The woman carefully passed
the bundle to Kylie. Lulu wondered what
animal could be hidden inside.

Kylie waved to Lulu and Molly.

'Come and take a peek, girls,' Kylie
said. 'Look what Mrs Russell rescued up
on the Parkway.'

Lulu and Molly came closer. Kylie
peeled back the towel to reveal
a furry grey
creature curled
up in a ball.
A long thin
ear flicked
back and forth.

'It's a wallaby joey,' said Kylie in a low voice. 'She's an orphan. Her mother was hit by a car. Mrs Russell found the joey safe in her mother's pouch.'

'Oh,' said Lulu, feeling sad. 'The poor baby.'

'Is she all right?' asked Molly.

The joey wriggled. Kylie covered her up again in the towel.

'Dr Bell will check her over, but she seems fine,' said Kylie.

Kylie turned to Mrs Russell. 'We'll look after her. Thanks for bringing her in.'

Mrs Russell said goodbye and left. A client came out of the consulting room with her huge Great Dane. She came to the counter to pay. The Great Dane was limping and his back leg was shaved. Dad had operated on his leg last week and the dog was finally going home.

Lulu patted him. 'Glad you're walking better, Sultan,' she said.

Kylie smiled at Sultan's owner. 'I'll be right back. I just need to pop this wallaby joey away safely.'

Kylie beckoned to Lulu and Molly to follow.

'Lulu, can you please ask your dad if he could quickly check the joey in the hospital ward? Then I'll send the next patient in,' said Kylie.

Dr Bell came at once to see the wallaby. Slowly and carefully, he lifted the joey out of the towel and put her on the table. Lulu and Molly stood beside him. The joey kicked and struggled. Dad gently put his hand over her eyes and she settled. He checked her all over.

'She's had a nasty shock,' Dad said. 'She's dehydrated. But she's quite big and not injured. If we can get her feeding well in the first twenty-four hours, I think she'll be all right.'

Lulu and Molly smiled at each other.

Dad gave the joey an injection to

rehydrate her. Then he wrapped her up in the towel so only her head was peeking out. She looked at Lulu with big brown eyes.

'Can we look after her, Dad?' asked Lulu.

Dad nodded. 'We'll care for her for a few months. But only until she's old enough to go back into the wild.'

'Hurray,' cried Lulu.

'What would you like to call her?' asked Dad.

Lulu thought for a moment. She looked at the beautiful grey wallaby, curled in the white towel like a ball.

'I think I'll call her Mika,' said Lulu. 'Our Aboriginal friends told me it means moon.'

Molly nodded in approval. 'That's very pretty.'

40

'Well, girls,' said Dad with a grin, 'time for you to get to work to make Mika comfortable.'

Chapter 5

Maisie

With some help from Kylie, Lulu
and Molly made a pouch for Mika to
sleep in. It was made from an old blue
flannelette pillowcase. A heat pad
tucked under the pillowcase kept the
joey warm.

Kylie helped them to mix up a bottle
of special milk formula. Lulu carefully
offered the teat to Mika. The joey took
a few sips from the bottle but she wasn't
very hungry. She hid her head inside the
pillowcase.

Lulu wrinkled her nose in dismay. 'She doesn't want to drink, Dad.'

'Never mind,' said Dad. 'She'll take some more milk a bit later when she gets used to us.'

Dad hung the pouch on the side of a special pen with high walls. 'Time Mika had a little sleep,' he said.

Lulu and Molly set to work in the hospital ward. They made sure that all the animals had fresh water to drink.

A while later, Kylie popped her head around the door.

'Your dad is seeing a special patient you know,' she said. 'Would you like to come and see?'

'Is it Maisie?' Lulu asked, excited.

'It sure is,' said Kylie. 'Your dad's checking the unborn puppies.'

'Let's go,' squealed Molly.

Lulu and Molly raced to the consulting room. Lulu knocked on the door.

'Come in,' called Dad.

Lulu opened the door. Inside was Lauren with her mum and her brother. Lauren grinned at them.

'Hi, Dad,' said Lulu. 'Kylie said we could come and see Maisie.'

Lying up on the consulting room table was a big, fat black Labrador. She was panting even though it wasn't hot. Dad was using his stethoscope to listen to Maisie's heartbeat.

'Maisie made a big nest in the bottom of my wardrobe this morning,' said Lauren's mum, Kyra. 'She dragged in lots of clothes from the washing basket.'

Lulu smiled at the thought of Maisie making a big puppy nest from dirty

45

clothes. Dad took Maisie's temperature.

Lauren looked at Dr Bell, her eyes shining. 'Do you think she will have the puppies this weekend?'

'I think Maisie is in for a very busy night tonight,' said Dr Bell. 'By the look of her, there will be at least eight.'

Maisie looked at Lulu with big, dark eyes. She looked very uncomfortable with her swollen tummy.

'How wonderful,' said Lulu. 'Can Molly and I come to visit after they are born?'

'Of course,' said Kyra. 'Maisie and the babies will need lots of peace and quiet for a while. But I'm sure she wouldn't mind a little visit.'

Dr Bell asked Kyra some questions to make sure she had everything ready for the new puppies.

'Ring me if you have any worries,' said Dad. 'We'll be home all evening.'

'Thanks so much, Dr Bell,' said Kyra. 'We'll let you know how she goes.'

Dr Bell carefully lifted Maisie down from the consulting table. He stroked her head. 'It's my pleasure.

Maisie will make a beautiful mother.'

Kyra took Maisie's lead and headed towards the door. Maisie waddled slowly, huffing and panting. Lauren's brother Justin followed.

'Come on, Lauren,' her mum said. 'Time to take Maisie home.'

Lulu looked wistful. 'I wish we could be there when they are born,' she told

Lauren. 'You're going to have such an amazing night.'

Lauren's face glowed with excitement. 'It's going to be the best night ever.'

Chapter 6

The Pyjama Party

 Lulu and Molly went home for lunch. Mum had made a big platter of sandwiches. Rosie, Sam and Gus had built a huge castle out of blocks in the middle of the kitchen floor.

Rosie jumped up from her chair as soon as she had finished eating. 'Is it time for the pyjama party to start?'

Lulu wrinkled her nose. 'We've only just had lunch!'

'Yes, but I can't bear to wait any more,' complained Rosie. 'You and Molly have been ages.'

Mum laughed. 'Why not? Why don't you set up all the beds now? Then you can get into your pyjamas and play some games.'

Rosie giggled with delight. Everyone set to work in the lounge room.

They pulled out mattresses, pillows and sleeping bags. Rosie carried in the dog beds. Molly put Ebony's basket near the fireplace. Almost the whole floor was covered. It was like camping.

Gus carried out all his soft toys — bears, puppies, bunnies, lambs and a huge green crocodile. He piled them up on his mattress until there was no room on the bed for Gus. Sam's bed was the opposite — perfectly neat and tidy.

The children took it in turns to have baths and change into their nightwear. Mum got into the spirit too. She changed into her nightie and slippers, even though it was the middle of the afternoon.

Lulu wore her favourite shortie PJs with her floppy-eared bunny slippers. Rosie wore a long white nightdress that nearly reached her ankles.

She had a circlet of orange roses on her hair. Molly and Sam had matching stripy flannelettes.

Gus came bounding out of his room. He had changed out of his bug boy costume into his all-in-one tiger suit. He even had black texta stripes drawn on his cheeks.

Lulu put her hand on her hip. 'Gus, what have you done to your face?'

'Grrrr,' growled Gus. 'Gussie got tiger whiskers.'

Lulu and Molly laughed.

'That texta won't wash off for days, honey bun,' said Mum,

with a sigh. 'Looks like we'll have a tiger on our hands for a while.'

Then all the kids lay on the kitchen floor to play board games.

Ebony the kitten loved playing too. She dived on the board, scattering cards everywhere. She pounced on the pieces and whacked them across the floor.

'*Ebony,*' cried Rosie. 'She's mucked up my cards *again*.'

'Naughty Ebby,' said Gus. He jumped up and curled his fingers like claws. He roared at her like a tiger.

Ebony ignored him. She stole Lulu's playing piece and shot it under the sideboard with a sneaky sideswipe.

Molly jumped up and caught the cheeky black kitten. She kissed the top of her furry head.

'It's a shame Ebony's so small,' said

Molly. 'She'd make a great soccer player.'

'I think we'd better lock Ebony in our room,' said Lulu with a sigh. 'Otherwise we'll never finish our game.'

When the vet hospital closed, Dad came home. He carried a pale-blue bundle and a baby's bottle full of milk.

'I have a very important job for you girls,' said Dad. 'We have an orphan joey to feed.'

'Poor Mika,' said Lulu. 'I hope she drinks the milk this time.'

'Everyone needs to be very quiet and calm,' warned Dad. He looked at Gus and Rosie. 'Understand?'

The kids all nodded. Rosie put the dogs outside so they wouldn't frighten the wallaby.

Molly sat on the couch and Dad placed the joey on her lap. Mika was

curled up inside
her flannelette
pillowcase, so she
felt safe and warm.

Dad showed
Lulu how to cover
the joey's eyes so
she wouldn't get
frightened. Lulu
sat beside Mika and fed her special milk
from the bottle. This time the joey was
hungry. She butted her head against
Lulu's hand as she sucked on the teat.

'She's drinking,' whispered Lulu. 'She's
going to be all right.'

Sam, Rosie and Gus sat on the floor
and watched. When the bottle was empty,
Mika did a somersault and disappeared
inside her pillowcase. Only her tail
poked out.

'That will keep her going for a few hours,' said Dad. 'I'll get up and feed her during the night.'

Dad hung Mika's pouch from a doorknob in Mum's art studio where she would be safe.

'Mika certainly was hungry,' said Lulu. She held up the empty bottle.

'Tiger hungry too,' declared Gus.

Mum laughed. 'I have just the right food for hungry tigers,' she said.

For afternoon tea, Mum made a special picnic with teensy, tiny cupcakes. There was a little teapot filled with apple juice and toy teacups. They had the picnic out in the garden, on a rug under the frangipani tree.

Most of the animals joined in too. There was Flopsy the bunny, the four fluffy ducklings, Ebony, Pickles and the two dogs. Rosie tried to make Pepper the cat join in but she stalked off in disgust.

As night fell, they played hide and seek in the dark with a torch. Asha and Jessie had to stay in the kitchen or they would sniff everyone out in seconds.

Gus found the best hiding spots but he could never wait to be found. He'd jump out way too soon, shouting, 'Here I am.'

Sam was good at hiding because he was quiet and patient. In the last game, Lulu, Molly and Rosie searched high and low for him for ages.

Molly finally found him wedged in the tiny space under the sofa. Ebony had given her a clue. The kitten kept darting back and forth under the sofa, patting Sam's glasses.

'There you are,' cried Molly. 'I thought we'd never find you.'

'I think Sam was the very best at hiding,' said Lulu.

Sam smiled a big grin. 'I like playing hide and seek here. There are so many secret spots.'

Chapter 7

Bed Time

Dad lit a fire in the fireplace and everyone sat around it. The kids were cross-legged on the mattresses on the floor. Dad had grilled meat patties on the barbecue to make burgers. They ate around the fire, as if they really were camping. Asha loved lying as close to the heat as she could get.

Dad told corny jokes.

'Why can't the elephant use a computer?' asked Dad.

'*Ellypant's* got no hands,' said Gus.

'No, because he's scared of the mouse,' said Dad.

'Ooooh,' groaned Mum and Lulu together.

Afterwards, they toasted marsh-mallows on long sticks over the flames. Dad looked after the fire. Sam and Gus toasted two marshmallows at a time until they were soft and gooey.

'*Dulishus,*' said Gus. He had pink and white streaks all over his face.

Molly wriggled back against the sofa. 'This is so much fun,' she said.

Sam yawned. Soon Rosie and Gus were yawning too. Dad put the fireguard over the fireplace. The flames had died away so there was just a pile of gently glowing coals. Asha turned around on her bed three times. She flopped down, her head on her paws.

Ebony chased her tail around and around until she fell over.

'I think it's time to clean your teeth. Then we can tuck you all into your sleeping bags,' said Mum. 'You've had a big day.'

Lulu felt disappointed. It couldn't possibly be bedtime yet. There was still so much fun to be had.

'I'm not tired,' complained Lulu.
'I can stay up for hours yet.'

'Me too,' said Rosie. She rubbed her eyes. Her circlet of roses slipped sideways.

'Time for bed, girls,' said Mum with a smile.

She took the circlet off Rosie's head and put it on the sideboard.

'Can you read us a story first, please, Mum?' begged Rosie. 'Can you read us the one about Fergus the frog?'

'All right, honey bun,' said Mum.

'Teeth first, then meet back here for a story and a kiss.'

All the kids raced off to the bathroom. Mum read them all a story and then another one and another one.

'Just one more,' begged Rosie, as Mum finished the last page. 'Pleeease Mum, best-mum-in-the-world?'

Mum laughed. 'Oh Rosie, you are incorrigible.'

'*Incorra-what?*' asked Rosie.

'Incorrigible,' replied Mum, stroking back Rosie's hair. 'Very, *very* cheeky and naughty.'

Mum kissed them all. Sam looked around at everyone with big eyes. He took his glasses off. Mum put them safely up on the mantelpiece.

'Are you all right, Sam?' asked Mum.

Sam nodded, so Mum turned out the light and crept out.

There was silence for a moment. Lulu could hear the comforting sound of Mum and Dad talking in the kitchen through the open door.

'Goodnight, everyone,' whispered Lulu.

'Goodnight, Lulu,' chorused Molly, Rosie and Gus.

Lulu thought she heard a sniffling, snuffling sound coming from Sam's bed. She sat up.

'Sam, would you like me to tell you a story?' asked Lulu.

There was a stifled sob and a hiccup. 'Yes, please, Lulu,' said Sam.

So Lulu whispered a story in the darkness. A story of dragons and a brave warrior princess who set off on a quest to save her tiger brother from the clutches of an evil witch.

Lulu finished the story. She thought everyone was asleep but she heard a funny little sound. She looked around in the soft glowing light from the fireplace, wondering what it was. Finally she saw Ebony curled up next to Sam, purring loudly. Lulu smiled and closed her eyes.

Chapter 8

Night Adventure

 Lulu woke up to the sound of the phone ringing in the kitchen. It was pitch-dark. *Who could be ringing this late?* wondered Lulu. It must be an animal emergency.

After hours, the vet hospital phone rang through to the kitchen. It was just in case someone urgently needed help.

Lulu heard Dad's voice answer the phone.

'Hello, Shelly Beach Vet Hospital. Dr Bell speaking,' said Dad.

There was a pause while Dad listened to the caller. 'I see,' said Dad. 'And is Maisie distressed?'

There was another pause. 'I think you had better bring her straight in. She may need a caesarean. I'll meet you at the vet hospital. See you soon.'

Dad tiptoed through the lounge room.

'Dad?' whispered Lulu sleepily. 'Is Maisie all right?'

Dad stopped. 'She's having trouble delivering her puppies. I need to take a look at her. You go back to sleep.'

Lulu tried to sleep. But now she was worried about Maisie and her puppies. At last, Lulu climbed out of her sleeping bag. She pulled on her bunny slippers and padded towards the vet hospital.

She pushed open the green door.

In the vet hospital, all the lights were
burning brightly. Lulu blinked in the
sudden light. The vet hospital seemed
strangely quiet at night-time.

Lulu checked each room. Dad was
not in the waiting room or the
consulting rooms. She heard a low
murmur of voices coming from the
operating theatre. Lulu peeked her head
around the door.

Dad was there, in the sterile green
gown and cap that he wore during
operations. He had thin plastic gloves on
his hands and a surgical mask over his
mouth. There were strong, warm lights
shining down.

Maisie was lying on the operating
table. She was unconscious and had
a breathing tube in her mouth. Her
stomach had been shaved and painted
with antiseptic.

Lauren and her mum were standing
by, looking anxious. Like Lulu, Lauren
was wearing her pyjamas.

'Perfect timing, Lulu,' said Dad. Lulu could hear the smile in his voice. 'Can you please scrub up, then fetch me a pile of sterile towels?'

Lulu washed her hands carefully, using the anti-bacterial soap at the sink. She fetched a pile of sterile towels from a cupboard and placed them on the benchtop. A moment later, Molly popped her head around the door.

'Sorry,' she said. 'I couldn't sleep either so I followed Lulu.'

'Come in, Molly,' invited Dad. 'We'll need all of you to help in a moment. I want to deliver the puppies as quickly as I can. Lulu will show you all what to do. She's done it before.'

Dad clamped a sterile cloth over Maisie's tummy. Beside the operating table was a trolley. On top, medical

instruments were laid out neatly.

Dad explained to Molly and Lauren.
'This operation is called a caesarean,'
he said. 'I make a small cut in Maisie's
tummy so I can pull out the puppies.
We need to do it quickly so that the
puppies are not affected too much by the
anaesthetic.'

Dad turned to Lulu. 'Are you ready to take delivery of the first pup?'

Lulu picked up a clean towel and held it out flat. Dad pulled a slippery puppy from Maisie's belly. He cleared away the sac and membranes, and cut the cord to detach it from its mother. Dad passed Lulu the first puppy. It was plump and black and lying perfectly still.

'This one's a fattie,' said Dad. 'A beautiful, healthy pup.'

'Hello, baby,' whispered Lulu.

Lulu's job was to rub the puppy with the towel to dry it and help it to breathe. She had to wipe the mucus from around its nose and mouth. It was important to work fast to get the puppy breathing as quickly as possible.

Dad passed another wrinkly puppy to Lauren, and then one to her mum Kyra.

Lulu rubbed her puppy. It lay unmoving and quiet in the towel. Lulu rubbed some more.

'Come on, little puppy,' whispered Lulu. 'Breathe. You have to breathe.'

Lulu rubbed a little harder. There was a tiny squeak. The puppy sucked in air. Lulu rubbed again. The puppy cried loudly, its eyes firmly shut.

'It's breathing,' squealed Lulu. Soon the pup was wriggling and squirming, its paws scrabbling in the air.

'Good work, Lulu,' said Dad. 'Pop it in the warming box. I have another one ready to go.'

Lulu laid the puppy in a special box under a heat lamp to keep it warm.

Dad passed her another puppy to rub. This one was smaller and a pale gold colour. The others were also working hard to revive their puppies.

'Mine's not breathing,' said Lauren. She sounded like she might cry.

'Just rub a little bit harder,' suggested Lulu. Lulu showed Lauren what to do, and the puppy took a sharp breath.

Soon the operating theatre was filled with the sound of squeaks and cries as the Labrador puppies began to breathe on their own.

'Eleven puppies,' said Dad. 'No
wonder Maisie was looking so big.'

Dad started work on sewing up the
cut in Maisie's tummy. Lulu worked
on her third puppy. Soon that pup was
breathing too.

Lulu gazed down at the warming box.
There were eleven fat puppies lying side
by side. Seven were golden Labradors
like their father and four were black

like Maisie. They mewled and whined, searching for their mother.

Lauren, Molly and Lulu grinned at each other with delight.

'Look at them,' said Lulu. 'Aren't they gorgeous? I'm sooooo glad the puppies were born in the middle of our pyjama party.'

Chapter 9

Midnight Feast

Maisie was still in a deep sleep.

'Poor Maisie,' said Lauren, her
forehead crinkled. 'Will she be all right?'

Dad pulled off his surgical gloves, cap
and mask. He beamed at the girls.

'She'll be fine, I promise you,' said
Dad. 'It will just take a little while for her
to wake up.'

Dad carefully lifted Maisie off the
operating table. He gently put her in

a large wooden box. It was lined with towels and newspaper. Maisie whimpered in her sleep.

One by one, the girls lifted the puppies and carefully placed them in the box beside Maisie. The pups snuggled up beside their mother. Some of them began to suckle. Dad turned on a heat lamp to keep Maisie and the puppies warm.

At that moment, Mum came in to check how things were going. She leaned over the puppy box and admired the babies.

'Puppies all delivered safe and well,' said Dad. 'But we need to stay here for a while and keep a close watch on Maisie. It will take an hour or so before she really wakes up.'

Mum looked at the girls in their pyjamas. She checked her watch.

'I think you and Molly had better go to bed, Lulu,' said Mum. 'It's the middle of the night.'

'Aw, Mum, no,' complained Lulu. 'Just a little bit longer. We want to help watch over the puppies.'

Molly and Lulu looked at Mum
pleadingly. Lauren looked from Lulu's
mum to her own mother.

'I suppose it wouldn't be a pyjama
party without a
midnight feast,' said
Mum. Her eyes
twinkled. 'I'll make
some snacks to keep
everyone going.
How's that for an
idea?'

'Great plan,' said
Dad. 'I'm starving.'

'Yes, *please*,' said
Lulu and Molly.
Kyra laughed.

'Midnight feast,
then bed – okay?
Kyra and Lauren,

would you like to join us?' Mum asked. They both nodded.

Mum came back a few minutes later, carrying a heavy tray. She was accompanied by a sleepy-looking Sam.

'Look who woke up,' said Mum. 'Sam didn't want to miss out on the puppies.'

Sam smiled at Lulu and Molly, then at the puppies.

Mum had made mugs of foaming hot chocolate with a sprinkle of shaved chocolate on top. She had also brought a plate of home-made lemon cupcakes.

Everyone sat on chairs in the operating theatre. They sipped hot chocolate and nibbled on crumbly cupcakes.

Maisie started to stir slowly. The eleven puppies were happily suckling, their eyes closed.

'What a wonderful weekend,' said Lulu. 'The pyjama party, looking after Mika and eleven new puppies. What do you think, Sam? Didn't I tell you we'd have fun?'

Sam gave a super-big grin. He had a chocolate foam moustache on his top lip.

'I had the best weekend ever,' said Sam. 'Maybe Molly, Ebony and I can come for a pyjama party again soon?'

'Absolutely, Sam,' said Lulu. 'Pyjama parties are the best!'

Lulu Bell and the Tiger Cub

Year Three are going on an excursion to the zoo. Luckily the zoo vet is one of Dad's best friends, so Lulu and Molly and their friends get special treatment!

When a tiger cub gets into trouble and hurts its leg, the zookeepers have to take it to the hospital. The zoo vet sets to work with Lulu and Molly looking on. Will the tiger cub be okay?

Out now

Read all the Lulu Bell books

Lulu Bell and the Birthday Unicorn

Lulu Bell and the Fairy Penguin

Lulu Bell and the Cubby Fort

Lulu Bell and the Moon Dragon

Lulu Bell and the Circus Pup

Lulu Bell and the Sea Turtle

Lulu Bell and the Tiger Cub

Lulu Bell and the Pyjama Party

Lulu Bell and the Christmas Elf
November 2014

About the Author

Belinda Murrell grew up in a vet hospital and Lulu Bell is based on some of the adventures she shared with her own animals. After studying Literature at Macquarie University, Belinda worked as a travel journalist, editor and technical writer.

A few years ago, she began to write stories for her own three children – Nick, Emily and Lachlan. Belinda's books include the Sun Sword fantasy trilogy, timeslip tales *The Locket of Dreams*, *The Ruby Talisman* and *The Ivory Rose*, and Australian historical tales *The Forgotten Pearl*, *The River Charm* and *The Sequin Star*. Belinda is also an ambassador for Room to Read and Books in Homes.

www.belindamurrell.com.au

About the Illustrator

Serena Geddes spent six years working with a fabulously mad group of talented artists at Walt Disney Studios in Sydney before embarking on the path of picture book illustration in 2009. She works both traditionally and digitally and has illustrated eighteen books, ranging from picture books to board books to junior novels.

www.serenageddes.com.au